For River, who makes everything feel
brand new. R. B.

For Renate and Wilhelm
And with special thanks to my dear Julius, who
helped with creating the hand lettering. Y. R.

First American Edition 2017
Kane Miller, A Division of EDC Publishing

Text © 2016 Rachel Bright
Illustrations © 2016 Yu Rong

Published by arrangement with Walker Books Ltd, 87 Vauxhall
Walk, London SE11 5HJ

For information contact:
Kane Miller, A Division of EDC Publishing
PO Box 470663
Tulsa, OK 74147-0663
www.kanemiller.com
www.edcpub.com
www.usbornebooksandmore.com

Library of Congress Control Number: 2016934248

Printed in China
1 2 3 4 5 6 7 8 9 10

ISBN: 978-1-61067-551-2

Snowflake in My Pocket

Rachel Bright   illustrated by Yu Rong

Kane Miller
A DIVISION OF EDC PUBLISHING

Once upon a winter,

in a faraway place, the last few leaves
of an old, twisted oak tree rattled in the breeze.

Inside that oak tree, lived a very wise bear
and a very small squirrel.

Bear had seen a hundred seasons, maybe more.

And Squirrel? Well, he had only seen three.

Together they
explored the four corners
of the forest. And whatever
Bear did, Squirrel tried, too.

woooo-hoooo!
Splosh-splish!

Munch-munch!

Wherever they went,
Bear had always
been there before.
But somehow
it all felt brand
new again with
Squirrel by his side.

One icy night,
as their breath blew in clouds,
Bear whispered, "It's on its way."
"*What is?*" sniffed Squirrel.

"Oh ..." Bear puffed. "The snow."
Squirrel gasped. "Will it snow *tonight*?
Do you think that it *might*?"

But a bear can never be *exactly* sure when
the weather will change. He just knows that it will.

So Squirrel tried his very hardest to stay awake
ALL NIGHT, searching and searching the twinkling sky.
But sometime between one star and the next,

he accidentally drifted off into a flurry of dreams.

So when the morning shone through his window,
he woke with a fast-beating heart, *thumpety-thud*.

With a *squeak-squeeeedge*, he cleared a hole
in the frost to see and ...

oh!

There was *MAGIC* surrounding their tree!

The snow *had* come in the night,
but ... so had the sniffles for Bear!

A... A... A...CHOOO!

And a bear with the sniffles
must stay in his bed until he is better.

So Squirrel tucked him up, took a deep breath
and promised to have fun for both of them.

Crunch ...

crunch ...

Squirrel's footsteps were the only sound in the forest.

*Crunch ... crunch ... crumbletycrunchCRUNCH*CRUNCHCRUNCH!

He ran
and rolled!

He made snow angels ...

and snow bears!

It was the most *perfect* morning.

Well, *almost* perfect.
For nothing could be completely perfect
without Bear.

In the silvery stillness,
a wonderful thought
tumbled into
Squirrel's head ...

"I

could

CATCH

a snowflake ...

and take it home to Bear!"

He ran in happy circles,

as they fell,

catching the snowflakes

until

he found

the *perfectest* one.

Then he put it in his pocket and set off for home.

"Bear!" he called. "Are you there? You couldn't come to the snow, so I've brought the snow to you!" And he reached in his pocket ...

But where his snowflake used to be ...

there was
nothing
at all.

"Where has it
gone?" Squirrel
said, as Bear
took his paw.

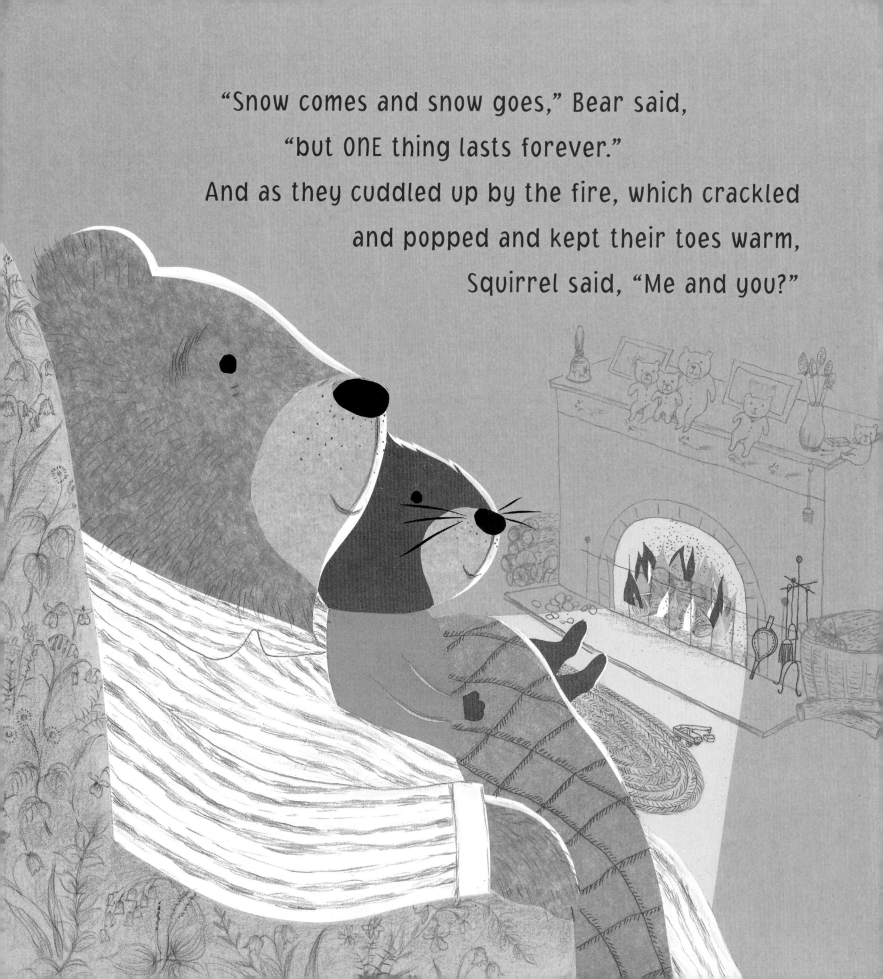

"Snow comes and snow goes," Bear said,
"but ONE thing lasts forever."
And as they cuddled up by the fire, which crackled
and popped and kept their toes warm,
Squirrel said, "Me and you?"

"Now and always," whispered Bear.